CARL'S CHRISTMAS

Carl's Christmas

ALEXANDRA DAY

FARRAR STRAUS GIROUX · NEW YORK

To Toby,
the real Carl

———————

Also by Alexandra Day

Carl Goes Shopping
Carl's Afternoon in the Park

"We're going to Grandma's and then to church.
Take good care of the baby, Carl."

Be our 1,000th customer and win this beautiful CHRISTMAS BASKET